This Little Tiger book belongs to:

_____

_____

_____

_____

PRESS THE PAGE
HEAR THE NOISE!

LITTLE TIGER PRESS
An imprint of Magi Publications
1 The Coda Centre, 189 Munster Road, London SW6 6AW
www.littletigerpress.com
First published in Great Britain 2010
This edition published 2011
Text by Stephanie Stansbie
Illustrations by Polona Lovsin
Text and illustrations copyright © Roar Publishing Limited 2010
A CIP catalogue record for this book is available from the British Library
All rights reserved • ISBN 978-1-84895-162-4
Printed in China
LTP/1800/0219/0511
2 4 6 8 10 9 7 5 3 1

Stephanie Stansbie • Polona Lovsin

# WHAT'S THAT NOISE, LITTLE MOUSE?

LITTLE TIGER PRESS
London

The moon was up, the night was still and Little Mouse
was half asleep. All at once, there came a noise –
a long and loud and trembling sound . . .

"What's that?" cried Mouse, now wide awake, holding his covers tight. But then he heard another noise, a steady tapping in the night . . .

Tick - tock!
Tick - tock!
Tick - tock!

Little Mouse crept out of bed and tiptoed from his room.
His heart was all a-flutter!

Outside, the wind was stirring in the trees,
shaking the leaves with a shivering breeze.
Through the hall window, crisp and clear,
came a bustling,

rustling,

whispering sound . . .

SSSSSSSSSSsssshhhhh

"Oh my goodness!" Little Mouse gasped,
and he scampered downstairs
as fast as he could!

hhhhhhhhhh!

Standing alone in the kitchen,
he couldn't believe his ears . . .

a wet and wobbly
dripping noise dribbled
in the dark . . .

Drip!
Drip!
Drip!

"It's a ghosty!"
Little Mouse cried,
and he ran and hid
in the cupboard.

The moonlight crept through the cupboard door,
casting shadows all around. Little Mouse heard
a grating sound – a creaking, squeaking,
scraping sound . . .

Crrreeeeeeaaaak!

"The ghosty's **coming to get me!**"
Little Mouse wailed.

He raced up the stairs and dived beneath
the covers. But then there came the
**worst** noise of all . . .

a rattling, chattering, clattering
sound – and it was heading straight towards
Little Mouse . . .

Rattle!

Rattle!

Rattle!

Shaking and quaking, and quivering
and shivering, Little Mouse let out the
loudest sound of all . . .

nhhhaaaaaahhhhhhhhh!

Quick as a flash, Mummy Mouse scampered into the room.

"What is it, little one?" she called.

"A g-g-ghosty!" Little Mouse cried. "It's louder than loud. Can you hear it?"

"I can hear Owly singing his song," said Mummy Mouse.

*Too-whoo!*
*Too-whoo!*

"And your little clock ticking to lull you to sleep."

*Tick-tock!*
*Tick-tock!*
*Tick-tock!*

**Sssssshhhhhhhhhhhhhh!**

"There's a breeze in the trees, wishing you good night,"

"a kitchen tap dripping,"

*Drip!*
*Drip!*
*Drip!*

"a cupboard door creaking,"

*Crreeeeeeeaaaak!*

"and your window panc rattling."

*Rattle!*
*Rattle!*
*Rattle!*

Mummy Mouse smiled . . .

"No ghosty, then," said Little Mouse. "I didn't think there was."
Mummy Mouse tucked him up and cuddled him close.
*"Sweet dreams, sleep tight, wish-a-mouse a quiet night!"*
she sang to him softly.

And soon the only noise to be heard in
the whole of the house . . .

was the **thunderous**
sound of a little mouse
snoring!

*Snoorre!*

*Snooorre!*

*Ssssnnoooorrrre!*

# YOU CAN'T MISS THESE VERY NOISY PICTURE BOOKS!

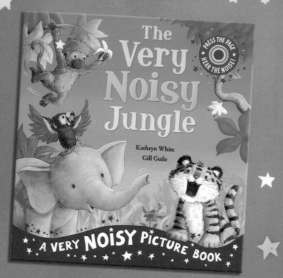

**The Very Noisy Jungle**
Kathryn White
Gill Guile
A VERY NOISY PICTURE BOOK

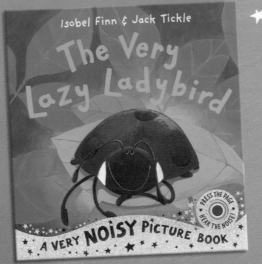

Isobel Finn & Jack Tickle
**The Very Lazy Ladybird**
A VERY NOISY PICTURE BOOK

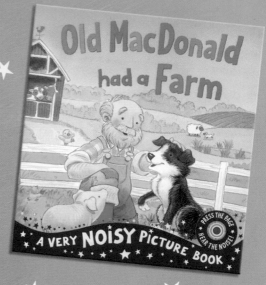

**Old MacDonald had a Farm**
A VERY NOISY PICTURE BOOK

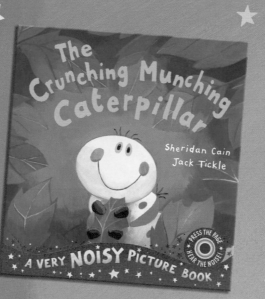

**The Crunching Munching Caterpillar**
Sheridan Cain
Jack Tickle
A VERY NOISY PICTURE BOOK

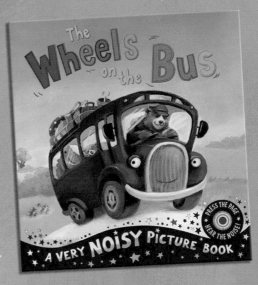

**The Wheels on the Bus**
A VERY NOISY PICTURE BOOK

For information regarding any of the above
titles or for our catalogue, please contact us:
Little Tiger Press, 1 The Coda Centre,
189 Munster Road, London SW6 6AW
E-mail: info@littletiger.co.uk • www.littletigerpress.com
Tel: 020 7385 6333 • Fax: 020 7385 7333